A Treasure Cove Story

WALT DISNEY'S

Peter Pan

From the motion picture *Peter Pan*
Based on the story by Sir James M Barrie
Illustrations by the Walt Disney Studio
Pictures adapted by John Hench and Al Dempster

In a quiet street in London lived the Darling family.
There were Father and Mother Darling, Wendy, Michael
and John, as well as the children's nursemaid, Nana
– a Saint Bernard.

At bedtime in the nursery, Wendy always told
wonderful stories about Peter Pan and Neverland,
a magical place with mermaids and fairies – and wicked
pirates, too.

John and Michael liked best of all to play pirates.
They had some fine slashing duels between Peter Pan
and his archenemy, the pirate Captain Hook.

Father Darling did not like this kind of play. He
blamed it on Wendy's childish stories of Peter Pan.

'It is time for Wendy to grow up,' decided Father Darling. 'This is your last night in the nursery, Wendy girl.'

All the children were much upset at that. Without Wendy, there would be no more stories of Peter Pan!

That very evening, who should come to the nursery but Peter Pan and a fairy named Tinker Bell! It seemed Peter had been out looking for his lost shadow. When he overheard that Wendy was to be moved from the nursery, he hit upon a plan.

'I'll take you to Neverland with me, to tell stories to my Lost Boys!' he decided as Wendy sewed his shadow back on.

Wendy thought that was a lovely idea – if Michael and John could go, too. So Peter Pan taught them all to fly – with happy thoughts and faith and trust, and a sprinkling of Tinker Bell's pixie dust. Then out the nursery window they sailed, heading for Neverland, while Nana barked frantically below.

Back in Neverland, Captain Hook was grumbling about Peter Pan. You see, once, in a fair fight long ago, Peter Pan had cut off one of the pirate captain's hands, so that he had to wear a hook instead. Then Pan threw the hand to a crocodile, who enjoyed the taste of Hook so much that he had been lurking around ever since, hoping to nibble at the rest of him. Fortunately for the pirate, the crocodile had also swallowed a clock. He went *ticktock* when he came near, which gave a warning to Captain Hook.

Now, as Captain Hook grumbled about his young enemy, there was a call from the crow's nest.

'Peter Pan ahoy!'

'What? Where?' shouted Hook, twirling his telescope around in the sky. And then he spied Peter and the children pausing for a rest on a cloud. 'Swoggle me eyes, it *is* Pan!' Hook gloated. 'Pipe up the crew… Man the guns… We'll get him this time at last!'

'Oh, Peter, it's just as I dreamed it would be
– mermaid lagoon and all,' Wendy said as a cannonball
ripped through the cloud beneath their feet.
'Look out!' cried Pan. 'Tinker Bell, take Wendy and
the boys to the island. I'll stay here and draw Hook's fire!'

Away flew Tinker Bell, as fast as she could go. In her naughty little heart, she hoped the children would fall behind and be lost. She was especially jealous of the Wendy girl, who seemed to have won Peter Pan's heart.

Straight through the Neverland jungle Tink flew, down into a clearing beside Hangman's Tree. She landed on a toadstool, bounced to a shiny leaf and *pop!* a secret door opened for her in the knot of the old hollow tree.

Zip! Down a slippery tunnel Tink slid. She landed at the bottom in an underground room – the secret house of Peter Pan.

Ting-a-ling! she tinkled, trying to awaken the sleeping Lost Boys.

At last, rather grumpily, they woke up and stretched as they listened to Tinker Bell.

'What? Pan wants us to shoot down a terrible Wendy bird? Lead us to it!' they shouted and out they hurried.

When Wendy and Michael and John appeared, flying wearily, the Lost Boys tried to pelt them with stones and sticks – especially the Wendy bird. Down tumbled Wendy, all of her happy thoughts destroyed – without them no one can fly.

'Hurray! We got the Wendy bird!' the Lost Boys shouted.

But then Peter Pan arrived. How angry he was when he discovered that the boys had tried to shoot down Wendy, even though he had caught her before she could be hurt.

'I brought her to be a mother to us all and to tell us stories,' he said.

'Come on, Wendy,' said Peter. 'I'll show you the mermaids. Boys, take Michael and John to hunt some Indians.'

So Peter and Wendy flew away and the boys marched off through the forest, planning to capture some Indians. There were wild animals all around, but the boys never thought to be afraid and not a creature harmed them as they went through the thick woods.

'First we'll surround the Indians,' John decided. 'Then we'll take them by surprise.'

John's plan worked splendidly, but it was the Indians who used it. Disguised as moving trees, they quietly surrounded the boys and took *them* by surprise!

Soon, bound with ropes, the row of boys marched away,
led by the Indians to their village on the cliff.

'Don't worry, the Indians are our friends,' the Lost Boys said,
but the chief looked stern.

Meanwhile, on the other side of the island, Wendy and Peter
were visiting the mermaids in their peaceful mermaid lagoon.
As they were chatting together, Peter suddenly said, 'Hush!'

A boat from the pirate ship was going by. In it were wicked
Captain Hook and Smee, the pirate cook. And at the stern, all
bound with ropes, sat Princess Tiger Lily, daughter of the Indian
chief.

'We'll make her talk,' sneered Captain Hook.

'She'll tell us where Peter Pan lives, or we'll leave her tied
to slippery Skull Rock, where the tide will wash over her.'

But proud and loyal Tiger Lily would not say a single word.

Peter and Wendy flew to Skull Rock. Peter, by imitating Hook's voice, tried to trick Smee into setting Tiger Lily free. That almost worked, but Hook discovered the trick and came after Peter with his sword. Then what a thrilling duel they had, all over the rocky cave where Princess Tiger Lily sat with the tide up to her chin!

Peter won the duel and rescued Tiger Lily just in the nick of time. Then away he flew to the Indian village, to see the princess safely home. And Wendy went along behind.

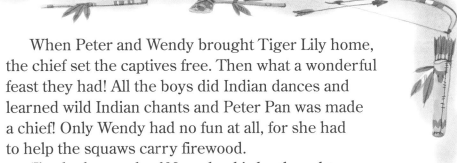

When Peter and Wendy brought Tiger Lily home, the chief set the captives free. Then what a wonderful feast they had! All the boys did Indian dances and learned wild Indian chants and Peter Pan was made a chief! Only Wendy had no fun at all, for she had to help the squaws carry firewood.

'I've had enough of Neverland,' she thought grumpily. 'I'm ready to go home right now!'

While the Indian celebration was at its height, Smee the pirate cook captured Tinker Bell and took her back to the pirate ship. He presented Tink to Captain Hook.

'Ah, Miss Bell,' said Hook sympathetically, 'I've heard how badly Peter Pan has treated you since that scheming girl Wendy came. How nice it would be if we could kidnap her and take her off to sea to scrub the decks and cook for the pirate crew!'

Tink tinkled happily at the thought.

'But, alas,' sighed Hook, 'we don't know where Pan's house
is, so we cannot get rid of Wendy for you.'

Tink thought this over. 'You won't hurt Peter?' she asked,
in solemn tinkling tones.

'Of course not!' promised Hook.

Then she marched to a map of Neverland and traced
a path to Peter's hidden house.

'Thank you, my dear,' said wicked Captain Hook, and he
locked her up in a lantern cage and went off to capture Peter Pan!

That night, when Wendy tucked the children into their beds in the underground house, she talked to them about home and Mother. Soon they were all so homesick that they wanted to leave at once for home. Wendy invited all the Lost Boys to come and live with the Darling family. Only Peter refused to go. He simply looked the other way as Wendy and the boys told him goodbye and climbed the tunnel to Hangman's Tree.

Up in the woods near Hangman's Tree waited
Hook and his pirate band. As each boy came out,
a hand was clapped over his mouth and he was quickly
tied up with ropes. Last of all came Wendy. *Zip, zip,*
she was bound up too and the crew marched off with
their load of children, back to their pirate ship.

'Blast it!' muttered Hook. 'We still don't have Pan!'

So he and Smee left a wicked bomb, wrapped as
a gift from Wendy, for poor Peter to find. Very soon,
they hoped, Peter would open it and blow himself
straight out of Neverland.

On the pirate ship, Captain Hook demanded that Wendy and the boys become pirates.

'Never!' Wendy cried.

'Then you shall be the first to walk the plank, my dear,' said Hook.

In the excitement, no one noticed that Tinker Bell escaped and flew off.

Wendy said goodbye, bravely walked along and off the long narrow plank and disappeared.

Everyone listened, waiting for a splash, but none came! Then they heard a familiar sound. It was Pan! Warned by Tinker Bell, he had arrived just in time to scoop up Wendy in midair and fly her to safety.

'This time you have gone too far, Hook,' Peter cried.

He swooped down from the rigging, all set for a duel. And what a duel it was!

While they fought, Tinker Bell slashed the ropes that bound the boys, and they fought the pirates, forcing them to jump overboard and row away in their boat. Then Peter knocked Hook's sword overboard and Hook jumped too. When the children last saw the wicked Captain Hook, he was swimming for the boat, with the crocodile *ticktocking* hungrily behind him.

Peter Pan took command of the pirate ship. 'Heave those halyards. Up with the jib. We're sailing to London,' he cried.

'Oh, Michael! John!' cried Wendy. 'We're going home!'

And sure enough, with happy thoughts and faith and trust, and a liberal sprinkling of pixie dust, away flew that pirate ship through the skies till the gangplank was run out to the Darlings' nursery windowsill. But now that they had arrived, the Lost Boys did not want to stay.

'We've sort of decided to stick with Pan,' they said.

So Wendy, John and Michael waved goodbye as
Peter Pan's ship sailed off through the sky, taking the
Lost Boys home to Neverland, where they still live today.

Treasure Cove Stories

Book list may be subject to change.